The Picture Man

By Julia Taylor Ebel

Illustrated by Idalia Canter

2009

Parkway Publishers, Inc.
Boone, North Carolina

Library of Congress Cataloging-in-Publication Data

Ebel, Julia Taylor.
The picture man / by Julia Taylor Ebel ; illustrated by Idalia Canter.
p. cm.
Includes bibliographical references.
Summary: An Appalachian farm girl and her brother have their pictures made by a traveling photographer in the 1940s. Includes facts about "picture men," early photography, and instructions for making a shoebox camera.
ISBN 978-1-933251-63-9 (hard cover)
[1. Photography--History--Fiction. 2. Farm life--Appalachian Region, Southern--Fiction. 3. Appalachian Region--History--20th century--Fiction.] I. Canter, Idalia, ill. II. Title.
PZ7.E165Pi 2009
[E]--dc22
2008039560
Printed in Mexico

Book design and color enhancement by Aaron Burleson, spokesmedia

In memory of Helen
To Joel and Rebecca
and to Jonathan, a new generation
—JTE

To my husband, Tom,
always "the wind beneath my wings,"
and with thanks to the Creator of my artist's eye
—IC

Acknowledgments

With gratitude to Helen Hardin Hovis Crenshaw, whose photograph of herself on Nell, the farm horse, inspired this book. The picture intrigued me from the moment I saw it. The photographer is unidentified. Thanks to Larry Hovis and Nancy Hovis Brown for permission to use this photograph. Thanks to William B. Becker of The American Museum of Photography for offering such helpful information in response to my questions about cameras and photographic history.

Thanks to Ralph E. Lentz II, who helped me understand the important role of picture men in keeping the story of Appalachian people. I appreciate his permission to use photographs taken by his step-great-grandfather, Willie Trivett, picture man.

Thanks to my publisher, Rao Aluri, for seeing the importance of keeping our rich personal histories, and to my book designer, Aaron Burleson, who has taken the best from Idalia and me and made it beautiful.

When the picture man came
rattling up the rough road
through the mountains,
I was out running in the field—
barefoot—
turning cartwheels
by the corn field.

Mama
was on the porch,
snapping beans we'd just picked,
beans she'd soon be canning
for winter meals.

When the picture man came,
a cloud of dust
from his car
rolled across the field.
Daddy and Junior
were digging potatoes
but paused to look up.

The picture man carried his camera
as he walked on out to Daddy.
He looked across the field
toward me
and then back at Daddy.
We didn't get many visitors
on the farm,
so I ran over
to see what was going on.

When the picture man came,
Daddy stood,
resting his hand on his hoe handle.
They talked about farming awhile—
about bean crops,
about how the rain last Tuesday
was mighty welcomed
after a dry spell.

Junior was trying
to size up that fancy camera
the man toted like a suitcase.
I sidled up close to him.

"How does this thing work?"
I asked.

The picture man
showed us his camera
and some fine pictures
he had already taken.

"The man's offering
to take your picture,"
Daddy said.
"Yours and Junior's."

"I reckon that's all right,"
I said.

Junior nodded
and grinned.

Mama'd figured out
what was going on.
She held up my Sunday dress
and Junior's good shirt.
"Better dust off a bit
and put on
some better clothes,"
she hollered at us.

I brushed some dust
off my overalls.
"I'm just fine,"
 I called back.

Then the picture man
asked me where
I'd want my picture made.
So I started thinking.
Maybe by the apple tree.

Maybe sitting by the creek.

But then I knew.

"Come on, Junior,"
I said.

We headed to the barn
and came back with big old Nell,
our plow horse,
still harnessed from farm work.

Junior held onto the reins.
"Whoa, girl," Junior said softly.
"Steady now."

Daddy helped me
climb up on Nell.
That horse was tough,
but she was mighty tame.
She'd stand right still for me.

Slowly and gently,
I settled myself
on old Nell's smooth back—
just as I had done many times before.
I was taller than anybody around,
about as tall as the mountain itself.

"Ready,"
I said.
"Smile, Junior!
Smile, Nell!"

The picture man bent forward
behind that camera,
which he'd perched
on three skinny bird legs.
He peered at us
through the camera.

I waited,
waited.

"Ready!"
the picture man said.

And
Click!
the picture man
took our picture.

Photography and the Picture Men

Photography had its beginnings many centuries ago with the *camera obscura.* The *camera obscura* is an enclosed box (or dark room) with a small opening. An image is projected through the opening onto the opposite side within the box.

Photography made important strides during the 1820s and 1830s, when permanent pictures were first kept on metal and paper. In the 1800s, cameras were large, but by the early 1900s cameras became smaller, faster, and easier to use. Now, cameras smaller than a young child's hand can fit in a pocket and yet take clear pictures. Digital cameras offer adjustments of light, focus, color, and more; and digital photographs can be edited in various ways with a computer.

People in early photographs often look stiff. To be photographed in the mid 1800s, a person had to sit motionless for as long as six minutes. As cameras improved, photographers could make pictures more quickly. The cumbersome view camera, used by earlier photographers, unfolded from a box to sit on a tripod. To focus the image, the photographer peered at a ground-glass plate in the camera while covering his head and the back of the camera with a dark cloth.

While view cameras remained in use, smaller, more portable folding cameras were available by the early 1900s. In 1900, Kodak made a small box camera, called the Brownie. It sold for $1.00 and was designed for personal use. Cameras such as the Brownie made home photography possible for persons who could afford the camera and the film processing.

Since the mid 1800s, photographers have captured the faces of America. Traveling photographers have shown us cowboys and farmers, immigrants and migrants workers. They have shown us the West and they have shown us war.

But some of the truest images of American people come from the picture men. These photographers often had other work, such as farming, but earned extra money by taking pictures. Picture men traveled—by foot, horseback, or car—within their communities to photograph people. Sometimes people came to the picture man's home.

Photographs made by the picture men went into family albums and on mantels. The public seldom has seen the pictures, yet these photographs, along with snapshots from personal cameras, show people as they saw themselves.

The photograph in the story, taken in the mid 1940s, shows Helen and Eddie Hardin at their family's Appalachian Mountain farm near Boone, North Carolina. The photographer is unknown, but Helen recalled his talking with her father about farming. The quality of the photograph suggests that the photographer knew his craft. Perhaps he was a picture man.

Signs of Photography by a Picture Man

- Photographs are taken outdoors.
- Subjects are posed. Hands may be placed together or holding an object to limit movement.
- Subjects may show something that is valuable: a car, a Bible, etc.
- Subjects often dress in their best clothes.
- Backgrounds are well chosen. A chair may be set in front of a natural backdrop, or a fabric backdrop may be draped behind the subjects.
- Attention is given to lighting and composition of the photograph.

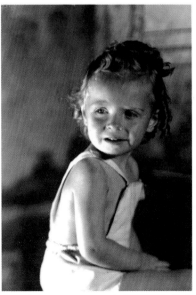

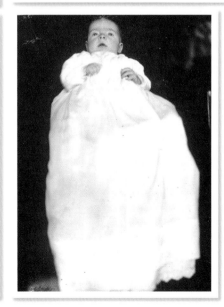

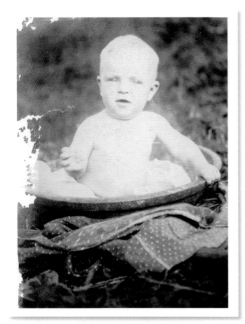

Photos by W. R. Trivett, photographer in rural Avery and Watauga Counties, North Carolina, between 1907 and the early 1940's

Resources

Lentz, Ralph E., II. *W. R. Trivett, Appalachian Pictureman*. Jefferson, NC, McFarland & Company, Inc., 2001.

Hawthorne, Ann, ed. *The Picture Man: Photographs by Paul Buchanan*. Chapel Hill, NC, The University of North Carolina Press, 1993.

Make a Shoebox Camera

      Make a pinhole in one end of a shoebox. Cover the hole with an opaque flap that can be lifted to allow light to reach the hole. Be certain that the flap keeps all light out when it is closed.

      Working in the dark, tape a piece of photographic paper on the opposite end inside the box. Close the box so no light can enter.

      Turn the pinhole toward the subject you wish to photograph. Lift the lens for a few seconds. The exposure time needed will vary with the amount of light on your subject. Keep the photographic paper away from light until it can be developed.

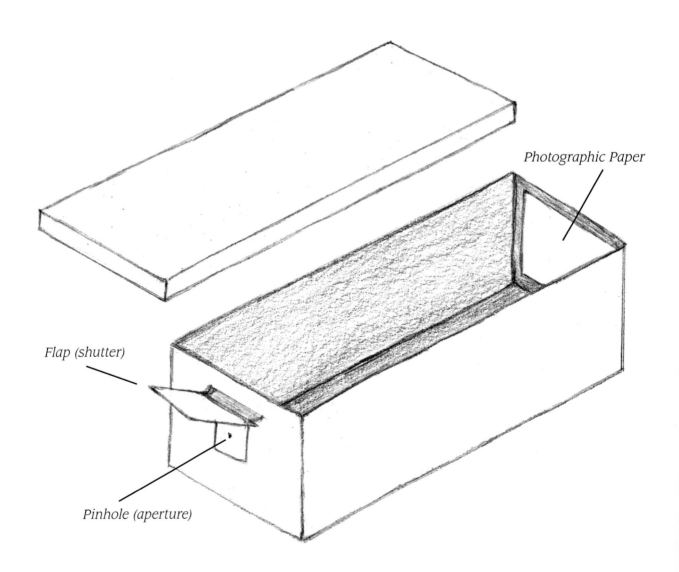

Photographic Paper

Flap (shutter)

Pinhole (aperture)